The big ingredient in a little bottle Cookbook

HarperCollins*Publishers*

First published in Australia in 1997
by HarperCollins*Publishers* Pty Limited
ACN 009 913 517
A member of the HarperCollins*Publishers* (Australia) Pty Limited Group

HarperCollins*Publishers*
25 Ryde Road, Pymble, Sydney, NSW 2073, Australia
31 View Road, Glenfield, Auckland 10, New Zealand
77–85 Fulham Palace Road, London W6 8JB, United Kingdom
Hazelton Lanes, 55 Avenue Road, Suite 2900, Toronto, Ontario M5R 3L2
and 1995 Markham Road, Scarborough, Ontario M1B 5M8, Canada
10 East 53rd Street, New York NY 10032, USA

National Library of Australia Cataloguing-in-Publication data:

The big ingredient in a little bottle cookbook: ANGOSTURA® aromatic bitters.
Includes index.
ISBN 0 7322 57824.
1. Cookery (Liquors). 2. Beverages. I. ANGOSTURA® aromatic bitters.

641.625
Concept: Sheer Rhetoric
Gourmet recipes created by Joan Campbell for Vogue Entertaining
Weight Watchers
Association of Professional Chefs and Cooks
ANGOSTURA® Limited, Port of Spain, Trinidad, W.I.
Swift and Moore Pty Ltd
Photography Andrew Elton – pages 11 to 21; George Seper – pages 25 to 41
Food Stylist: Karen Cotton – pages 11 to 21
Home Economist: Lynne Mullins – Pages 11 to 21
Illustrations by Steven Bray

9 8 7 6 5 4 3 2 1
99 98 97

The big ingredient in a little bottle Cookbook

HarperCollins*Publishers*

INTRODUCTION

Welcome to the taste of ANGOSTURA® aromatic bitters, The Big Ingredient in a Little Bottle. Many people already enjoy ANGOSTURA® in cocktails and marinades but its unique flavour has many more uses in your kitchen.

Whether you're planning a gourmet dinner party, a light and healthy lunch or a tempting dessert, the recipes we've gathered together are sure to add that something special to your menu.

ANGOSTURA® has a colourful history stretching over 170 years. Its creator, Dr Johan Siegert, was a surgeon in Simon Bolivar's army of liberation in Venezuela during the 1820s.

The doctor was searching for a healthy potion for his soldiers and the result of his work was a blend of herbs and spices which is now known as ANGOSTURA® aromatic bitters, named after the Venezuelan village where he lived.

When the Siegert family moved to Trinidad in the 1870s they took their recipe with them and ANGOSTURA® became one of the Caribbean Islands' most famous exports.

Thank you to Vogue Entertaining who have kindly given us permission to include some mouth-watering ANGOSTURA® recipes created by Joan Campbell.

Thank you also to Weight Watchers who have provided several recipes that are big on taste but low in calories.

ANGOSTURA® is rapidly becoming a favourite ingredient in many Australian restaurants. Our Chef's Selection features fabulous recipes from some innovative chefs.

We hope ANGOSTURA® aromatic bitters will become an essential ingredient in your kitchen.

THE CHEFS

MATTHEW GOUDGE

MEMOIR CAFÉ RESTAURANT
TURA BEACH, NSW

Matthew began his apprenticeship on the NSW south coast and then travelled overseas where he worked in various roles, including Chef de Partie and Sous Chef, at a range of London restaurants and studied the techniques and menus of chefs in and around Europe.

Upon returning to Australia, Matthew used his new found knowledge to tempt restaurant goers in Melbourne, working at Blakes, Scusa Mi, The Church and The Point. He has since returned to the south coast opening the Memoir Café — an informal BYO restaurant specialising in Australian cuisine with an Italian influence.

ANTONIO OZCAN

DEMI CHEF DE PARTIE
SYDNEY HARBOUR CASINO, SYDNEY, NSW

Antonio began his apprenticeship at the Sydney Turf Club and later worked at Sydney's Park Lane and Intercontinental Hotels before moving to the Sydney Harbour Casino. The casino has three restaurants, Jake's Grill, Astral and Spinnakers Buffet. More than 2500 people dine at the casino each day.

JUSTIN O'DONOUGHUE

CHEF DE PARTIE
HERIVEL'S RESTAURANT
HAWKESBURY LODGE RUM CORPS CONVENTION CENTRE, WINDSOR, NSW

Justin served his apprenticeship in various Sydney restaurants before gaining experience in function and conference work. He plans to travel overseas to gain additional experience which he hopes will complement his speciality — modern Australian cuisine.

RUSSELL CARTER

CHARTERS TOWERS
CONRAD JUPITERS CASINO
BROADBEACH, QLD

Russell has worked at Conrad Jupiters Casino since he began his apprenticeship in 1993. Charters Towers is a fine dining restaurant with an emphasis on Australian cuisine.

ALAN LENNON

1918 BISTRO AND GRILL
TANUNDA, SA

Alan began his apprenticeship in Adelaide in 1980. During his seven-and-a-half year tenure as head chef at The Rising Sun Inn, the restaurant won the industry award for Best Restaurant in a Hotel in South Australia.

In 1995 Alan and his wife, Jenny, took over the 1918 Bistro and Grill and have already received recognition, winning the American Express Best Restaurant Award in the Barossa Valley region. From its relaxed front garden to its warm and welcoming open fires 1918 is a restaurant for all seasons. Alan features a distinctive provincial menu prepared from local seasonal produce.

TIM KARRASCH

SHORES RESTAURANT
PELICAN BEACH RESORT
COFFS HARBOUR, NSW

Tim began his apprenticeship in Brisbane before moving to NSW where he qualified as a chef. He travelled overseas and worked in the UK before returning to Australia where he is now the Chef de Partie at Pelican Beach Resort. Shores Restaurant is à la carte with a strong emphasis on seafood.

CONTENTS

Chefs' Selection

Ocean Trout Cured with ANGOSTURA® aromatic bitters and Gin with Mustard and Dill Dressing

CURED OCEAN TROUT

- 15ml ANGOSTURA® aromatic bitters
- 60ml gin
- 2 sides ocean trout, scaled and boned
- 12 tablespoons rock salt
- 8 tablespoons caster sugar
- 4 teaspoons white pepper
- 4 sprigs fresh thyme

GARNISH: 1 Spanish onion, cut in rings; 100g deep-fried large capers; baby beetroot leaves

MUSTARD AND DILL DRESSING

- 2 teaspoons seeded mustard
- ½ teaspoon English mustard
- 4 teaspoons Dijon mustard
- 1 teaspoon caster sugar
- 1 teaspoon ANGOSTURA® aromatic bitters
- 1 egg yolk
- 150ml light olive oil
- 150ml vegetable oil
- 1 teaspoon chopped dill

Rub ANGOSTURA® and gin into the flesh of the fish. Mix salt, sugar, pepper and thyme. Place two thirds of spice mixture into a deep tray, put the fish on top, skin side up.

Place remaining mixture on top of the fish and place a tray over it with a light weight on top of the tray. Place in the refrigerator to cure for 30 hours, turning every 10 hours. When cured, remove the fish from the solution, wipe and wrap in plastic wrap until required. The fish will keep in the refrigerator for up to two weeks.

MUSTARD AND DILL DRESSING

Put the first six ingredients into a blender. Process. Slowly add the oils with the motor running. Remove from blender, place in a bowl and stir in chopped dill.

TO SERVE: Thinly slice cured trout from the tail end. Arrange on a bed of baby beetroot leaves. Drizzle dressing over the fish and garnish with thinly sliced red onion rings and fried capers.

SERVES 4 TO 6 AS AN ENTRÉE

Variation: Dressing can be served with smoked salmon or smoked trout.

Dish created by Matthew Goudge
Memoir Café Restaurant

Chicken Breast with Champagne and ANGOSTURA® aromatic bitters Beurre Blanc

4 x 250g chicken breasts
salt and pepper to taste
50g butter
100g chopped shallots
100ml champagne
20ml ANGOSTURA® aromatic bitters
100ml cream
50g julienne carrots
100g snap beans
100g bean sprouts
50g julienne red capsicum

Preheat oven to 160°C. Season chicken breasts and pan fry in butter till golden brown. Finish cooking in oven for 5–10 minutes. Sauté shallots, champagne and ANGOSTURA® in pan. Reduce sauce by half before adding cream. Simmer sauce.

In another pan lightly sauté carrots, beans, bean sprouts and capsicum. Finish sauce by stirring in knobs of butter.

TO SERVE: Place some of the vegetable panache in the centre of the plate. Place chicken breast on top and mask with sauce.

SERVES 4

Variation: Can also be served on a bed of pasta accompanied by a mixed leaf salad.

Dish created by Antonio Ozcan
Sydney Harbour Casino

Grilled Atlantic Salmon Fillet with Lemon Myrtle Crumble and ANGOSTURA® aromatic bitters Sauce

4 portions Atlantic salmon fillet
2 teaspoons ANGOSTURA® aromatic bitters
juice and zest of half a lemon
50ml white wine
80g softened butter
Seasoning

CRUMBLE
50g butter
30g sugar
1 teaspoon ANGOSTURA® aromatic bitters
110g plain flour
1 lemon myrtle leaf

Preheat oven to 190°C. Rub together butter, sugar, flour and 1 teaspoon of ANGOSTURA®. Add crushed lemon myrtle leaf. Seal upper side of salmon in pan, then turn over onto an oven tray, moulding a thin layer of crumble mix over the fillet. Place in oven to cook through (20–30 minutes) before setting aside to keep warm. Add wine and lemon juice to pan, place on low heat and whisk in butter. Simmer gently and then add seasoning, 2 teaspoons of ANGOSTURA® and blanched zest. While sauce is simmering place fish under grill to gratinate top of crumble.

TO SERVE: Place fillet in centre of plate and encircle with sauce. Garnish with chervil sprig and accompany with either a mesclun and cherry tomato salad with a light balsamic vinegar dressing or steamed asparagus, snow peas and broccoli.

SERVES 4

Dish created by Justin O'Donoughue
Herivel's Restaurant

Rack of Lamb with Pawpaw Salsa

4 racks lamb
250g pawpaw
150g Spanish (red) onion
2 cloves garlic
200g tomato
50ml champagne vinegar
50ml extra virgin olive oil
1 tablespoon chopped mint
5–10ml ANGOSTURA® aromatic bitters
salt and pepper to taste
sugar to taste
300g pontiac potatoes
300g Jerusalem artichokes (or sweet potato)
50g butter
50ml cream

Preheat oven to 220°C. Season the lamb well with salt and cracked pepper and seal quickly in a hot pan, then set aside on a rack for roasting.

Dice pawpaw into fine pieces and set aside. Chop Spanish (red) onion finely and grind the garlic. Skin and seed the tomato and dice finely. Mix these four ingredients in a bowl with the vinegar, olive oil, mint and ANGOSTURA® and then season to taste with salt, pepper and sugar. Boil potatoes and artichokes together until soft, then mash with butter and cream. Finish cooking racks of lamb in the oven to your liking, 8–10 minutes rare, 15–20 medium. Let lamb rest for five minutes.

TO SERVE: Place a portion of mash in the centre of each plate, cut the racks into cutlets and serve with the bones pointing upwards in the centre of the plate. Sprinkle pawpaw salsa around the outside in a ring encircling the meal.

SERVES 4

Variation: Can also be served with lamb jus.

Dish created by Russell Carter
Charters Towers

Orange and ANGOSTURA® aromatic bitters Pudding

PUDDING
4 oranges
240g softened butter
240g caster sugar
4 eggs
350g self-raising flour
pinch of salt
4–6 drops of ANGOSTURA® aromatic bitters

SAUCE
500g treacle or golden syrup
4 drops ANGOSTURA® aromatic bitters

Preheat oven to 165°C. Zest orange rind and place into stainless steel pan. Add juice from the oranges to the pan and cook on low heat until reduced by two thirds. Let cool. Place butter and caster sugar in a bowl and beat until light and creamy. Add eggs one at a time, mixing well. Sift flour and salt together and gradually add to creamed mixture. Mix well. Mix in orange reduction and ANGOSTURA®.

Separate mixture into 10 well-greased tin moulds or small baking tins. Place on tray in middle rack of oven for approximately 1 hour or until pudding is golden in colour and springs back when touched in centre. To heat sauce add ingredients and warm for 1 minute on high setting in microwave.

TO SERVE: Turn puddings out onto dishes and serve with sauce and double cream. Garnish with orange zest.

SERVES 10

Variation: Puddings can be cooked in advance and reheated in the microwave.

Dish created by Alan Lennon
1918 Bistro and Grill

ANGOSTURA® aromatic bitters and Raspberry Ice Cream Served in a Macadamia Chocolate Basket

3 egg yolks
¾ cup caster sugar
¾ cup milk
⅔ cup cream
500g fresh or frozen raspberries (puréed)
1–2 teaspoons ANGOSTURA® aromatic bitters
100g crushed roasted macadamia nuts
500g dark cooking chocolate

Whisk egg yolks and sugar until light and frothy. Set aside. Heat milk and cream in a double boiler until near boiling. Whisk in egg mixture, cook slowly over double boiler until mixture coats spoon. Allow to cool before stirring in puréed raspberries and ANGOSTURA®. Place mixture into ice cream maker and when frozen place in freezer.

Melt chocolate over water bath then add macadamia nuts. Mix well. Spread a small amount of the chocolate mixture onto a plastic sheet and shape over a cup or glass. Make sure chocolate is not too thick. Remove when set.

TO SERVE: Place chocolate basket onto plate and place a scoop of ice cream inside. Serve with cream and berry coulis or fresh raspberries and kiwi fruit. Garnish with mint.

SERVES 6

Dish created by Tim Karrasch
Shores Restaurant

Gourmet

Smoked Salmon Salad

1 small side of smoked salmon
1 or 2 bulbs of fennel, coarse outer leaves removed. Inside leaves should be finely julienned
3 Lebanese cucumbers, seeded and sliced very thinly
salt and freshly ground pepper

DRESSING
½ cup light olive oil
juice of half a lemon
1 teaspoon seeded French mustard
2 teaspoons ANGOSTURA® aromatic bitters
salt and freshly ground pepper

Arrange 5 slices of smoked salmon on each serving plate. Combine all the dressing ingredients. In separate bowls toss the fennel and cucumber with salt and pepper and some dressing.

Arrange a pile of fennel on top of the salmon, then add a layer of cucumber. Season with ground pepper and serve at once.

SERVES 4

Prawns on a Bed of Red and Yellow Capsicum, Okra and Zucchini

2 red and 2 yellow capsicum, skin peeled with a vegetable peeler, seeds and membranes removed, cut lengthwise in wide strips
butter
8 small zucchini, sliced in half, lengthwise
16 okra
500g green prawns, peeled and cleaned
1 tablespoon ANGOSTURA® aromatic bitters
juice of 1 lime
salt and freshly ground pepper

TO COOK THE VEGETABLES: Heat a little oil in a frying pan and cook the red and yellow capsicum strips until softened. Remove and keep warm. In a clean pan melt a little butter, add the zucchini strips and fry until just cooked. Remove and keep warm. Add more butter to the pan if needed and fry the okra until just cooked.

TO COOK THE PRAWNS: Melt a little butter in a frying pan, add the prawns and cook over high heat, tossing until they change colour and are cooked, about 3 minutes.

TO SERVE: Mix the lime juice and ANGOSTURA® together in a small bowl. Sprinkle the vegetables with salt and freshly ground pepper and arrange on the centre of each serving plate. Place prawns on top, sprinkle with the mixed lime juice and ANGOSTURA® and serve at once.

SERVES 4

Barbecued Prawns with Asian Flavours

MARINADE

3 tablespoons ANGOSTURA® aromatic bitters
4 tablespoons Thai sweet chilli sauce
1¼ cups pineapple juice
5 cloves garlic, peeled and crushed
4 tablespoons Thai fish sauce
1 cup peanut oil
1 cup coconut milk
1 tablespoon Hoi Sin sauce

PRAWNS

1kg green king prawns

TO SERVE

2 to 3 tablespoons plum sauce

MARINADE: Place all ingredients in a bowl and whisk together.

PRAWNS: Add the prawns to the marinade and marinate for 3 to 4 hours turning now and again. Thread the prawns on skewers. Reserve the marinade and set to one side. Grill prawns over the barbecue, turning from time to time until their colour changes and the prawns are cooked.

TO SERVE: Pour the marinade into a saucepan. Add the plum sauce, bring the mixture to the boil and simmer for a few minutes. Serve the prawns with the sauce and green salad.

SERVES 6

Caribbean Lamb

1 tablespoon oil
1 tablespoon butter
2 onions, peeled and sliced
1kg trim lamb, cubed
salt and freshly ground pepper
1½ cups chicken stock
¼ teaspoon ground cloves
2 cinnamon sticks
2 teaspoons grated ginger
2 tablespoons ANGOSTURA® aromatic bitters
juice of 1 lemon
½ cup cream
½ cup chopped sun-dried tomatoes
continental parsley, chopped roughly
saffron rice
roasted almonds

Heat the oil and butter in a frying pan and sauté the onion until brown. Remove the onion to a large saucepan, then fry the lamb in the frying pan until it is brown on all sides. Add the ANGOSTURA®.

Remove the lamb to the saucepan with the onions and add the salt, pepper, chicken stock, cloves, cinnamon and ginger. Cover and simmer for 30–40 minutes. Uncover, add the lemon juice and cook for a further 5 minutes. Add the cream and sun-dried tomatoes and bring to a simmer.

Cook rice until light and fluffy (approximately 10–12 minutes) then stir parsley through the rice.

TO SERVE: Pile some rice onto each serving plate and spoon the lamb on top. Sprinkle with roasted almonds and serve at once.

SERVES 6

Chicken on Rice and Chickpeas with an Orange Sauce

RICE AND CHICKPEAS

5 cups chicken stock
1½ cups basmati rice
170g bacon, rind removed, cut in thin strips
vegetable oil
1 onion, peeled and chopped
1 clove garlic, peeled and crushed
3 sticks celery, sliced crosswise
½ teaspoon fresh thyme leaves
pinch of chilli flakes
grated rind of 2 limes
2 x 380g tins chickpeas, drained
salt and pepper to taste

CHICKEN

9-12 chicken thigh fillets, halved, lengthwise
plain flour
vegetable oil

SAUCE

vegetable oil
1 tablespoon grated fresh ginger
1 clove garlic, peeled and crushed
grated rind of 2 oranges
1 cup orange juice
1 tablespoon brown sugar
3 tablespoons coconut cream
1 tablespoon ANGOSTURA® aromatic bitters

TO COOK THE RICE AND CHICKPEAS: Bring the chicken stock to the boil, add the rice and bacon strips. Boil the rice for 12 minutes. Drain and set aside. In a little vegetable oil, fry the onion, garlic, celery, thyme, chilli flakes and lime rind until soft. Add the chickpeas and heat. Add the rice and bacon and season to taste. Mix over low heat, cover and set aside.

TO COOK THE CHICKEN: Dust the chicken pieces lightly with flour. Pour a little vegetable oil into a large frying pan and fry the chicken pieces, on both sides, until golden.

TO MAKE THE SAUCE: Pour a little vegetable oil into a small saucepan and cook the ginger, garlic and grated rind over low heat until soft. Add the orange juice, brown sugar and coconut cream and bring to the boil. Remove from the heat and keep warm. Add the ANGOSTURA® just before serving.

TO SERVE: Place a mound of the rice mixture on each serving plate, add three to four pieces of the chicken, pour over the sauce and serve at once.

SERVES 6

Tamarillo and ANGOSTURA® aromatic bitters Ice Cream with Poached Tamarillos

POACHED TAMARILLOS

4 cups sugar
12 tamarillos, skin and stems left on
4 cups water

ICE CREAM

6 poached tamarillos, skin and stems removed
1 cup poaching syrup
2 tablespoons ANGOSTURA® aromatic bitters
1 litre good quality vanilla ice cream, softened slightly

TO POACH THE TAMARILLOS: Put the sugar and water in a saucepan and bring to a simmer, stirring until the sugar dissolves. Add the tamarillos and simmer until the flesh is cooked and has turned deep red. Transfer the tamarillos and syrup to a bowl and set aside to cool, then cover and chill in the refrigerator.

TO MAKE THE ICE CREAM: Put 6 poached tamarillos and poaching syrup in a blender and purée. Sieve to remove seeds, then mix the ANGOSTURA® into the purée. Mix the purée with the ice cream, then transfer to a covered container and store in the freezer until serving time.

TO SERVE: Slice the remaining chilled tamarillos in two, lengthwise, leaving the stems intact. Serve in individual dishes with a scoop of ice cream.

SERVES 6

Banana Ice Cream

3 large bananas
½ cup brown sugar
1½ tablespoons cream
1 tablespoon butter
few drops of vanilla extract
1 tablespoon ANGOSTURA® aromatic bitters
300ml thickened cream, whipped

Peel the bananas, chop roughly and place in a bowl. Cook the sugar, cream and butter together over low heat for about five minutes. Remove the pan from the heat and stir in vanilla, ANGOSTURA®, banana and cream.

Purée the mixture in a food processor, then freeze in an ice cream machine. Store in a covered container in the freezer until required. Drizzle ANGOSTURA® over ice cream and serve.

SERVES 6

Strawberry Tart

PASTRY

125g butter, cubed
pinch of salt
1½ cups plain flour
2 tablespoons iced water

FILLING

Mascarpone cheese
1 punnet strawberries hulled, halved and marinated in ¼ cup sugar and 1 tablespoon ANGOSTURA® aromatic bitters

PASTRY: Process the butter, flour and salt in a food processor until the mixture is like coarse breadcrumbs. Add the water and continue to process until the dough forms a ball. Wrap in plastic wrap and refrigerate for 30 minutes.

Roll out the dough on a lightly floured board and line a greased 20cm tart tin. Prick the bottom with a fork and bake in a preheated 190°C oven for 12 minutes or until the pastry is golden. Remove from the oven and leave to cool.

TO FILL AND SERVE: Fill the pastry case with Mascarpone. Arrange the marinated strawberries on top and serve.

SERVES 4 TO 6

ANGOSTURA

light
and
healthy

Green Vichyssoise with Tomato, Mint and ANGOSTURA® aromatic bitters

2 cups fresh or frozen peas
2 medium potatoes, sliced
2 medium onions, sliced
1 small iceberg lettuce, roughly chopped
5 cups chicken stock
2 tablespoons ANGOSTURA® aromatic bitters
seasoning to taste
500g ripe tomatoes
1 tablespoon lemon juice
10 mint leaves, finely chopped
8–10 mint sprigs for garnish

Place peas, potatoes, onions and lettuce in a large saucepan with stock. Stir in 1 tablespoon of ANGOSTURA® and bring to the boil, reduce heat and simmer until potatoes are cooked. Cool and purée, adjusting seasoning to taste. Pour into a bowl, cover and refrigerate until well chilled.

Chop tomatoes into fine pieces, transfer to a bowl and stir in lemon juice, remaining ANGOSTURA® and chopped mint. Cover and refrigerate until well chilled. Ladle Green Vichyssoise into serving bowls. Swirl tomato and bitters mixture through each serving, garnish with a sprig of mint.

SERVES 8

Variation: Soup can also be served hot.

Cucumber Wrapped Scallops

500g scallops or shelled prawns
1 teaspoon ANGOSTURA® aromatic bitters
1 tablespoon lime or lemon juice
2 tablespoons olive oil
4 telegraph cucumbers (as straight as possible)

Toss scallops in combined ANGOSTURA®, lime juice and oil. Cover and refrigerate overnight, stirring occasionally. (Marinade will 'cook' scallops, turning them white and opaque.)

Using a swivel-bladed vegetable peeler, remove skin from cucumber then peel thin ribbon lengths of cucumber and use them to encase the scallops, securing them with toothpicks.

Serve slightly chilled.

SERVES 6 TO 8

Sweet Potato Kebabs

300g white sweet potato
300g red sweet potato
1 x 440g can unsweetened pineapple rings
4 small Granny Smith apples, cored
2 teaspoons ANGOSTURA® aromatic bitters
1 tablespoon polyunsaturated margarine
1½ teaspoons cinnamon
¼ teaspoon nutmeg
2 tablespoons lemon juice

Boil sweet potatoes in their skins until just tender. Cool, peel and cut into wedges. Drain pineapple, retaining one third of a cup of juice. Cut each pineapple ring into 6. Cut each apple into 8 wedges. Thread pineapple and apple onto 12 skewers with sweet potato wedges.

Melt margarine in a saucepan and add ANGOSTURA® and retained pineapple juice. Stir. Add remaining ingredients and stir well. Brush mixture over kebabs. Grill or barbecue, basting frequently until cooked and golden brown and apple is just tender, approximately 15–20 minutes.

Serve as part of a barbecue or as an entrée on their own, garnished with sprigs of mint.

SERVES 6

Baked Red Snapper in Oyster Sauce

1 medium sized red snapper
1 tablespoon peanut oil
2 thin slices fresh ginger, finely chopped
1 clove garlic, crushed
1 tablespoon soy sauce
1 tablespoon oyster sauce
1 tablespoon ANGOSTURA® aromatic bitters
½ red capsicum, cut into strips
1 small carrot, cut into thin strips
1 tablespoon finely chopped onions
½ green capsicum, cut into strips
1 stick celery, finely diced

Prepare fish by removing eyes and trimming tail and fins. Pat dry and score skin at 2cm intervals to prevent shrinkage. Heat oil in a small saucepan over medium heat. Cook ginger, garlic and onions until tender. Add soy sauce, oyster sauce and ANGOSTURA®. Simmer for 1 minute. Arrange fish on lightly greased oven-proof dish. Brush with the sauce, retaining some for basting during cooking.

Bake in a preheated 180°C oven for 40–45 minutes or until fish flakes easily with a fork. Parboil vegetables and use to garnish fish prior to serving.

SERVES 4

Pork with Mango, Curry Sauce and Caramelised Apples

1 x 1.5kg pork neck
3 tablespoons ANGOSTURA® aromatic bitters
3 Granny Smith apples, cored and sliced
½ cup olive oil
2 cups roughly chopped mango
150ml cider vinegar
1 tablespoon honey
1 teaspoon curry powder

Trim pork of excess fat. Rub outside of meat with 1 tablespoon of ANGOSTURA® and sprinkle 1 tablespoon over the apples. Toss to thoroughly coat.

Heat 1 tablespoon of oil in a large frying pan and brown pork all over. Place pork in a baking dish, pour over pan juices and roast at 180°C for 1½ hours or until cooked. Wrap pork in foil. Cool and refrigerate until cold.

Sauté apples in pan juices until just soft, spoon into bowl, cover and refrigerate.

Combine mango, oil, vinegar, honey, curry powder and remaining tablespoon of ANGOSTURA® in a food processor and process until smooth.

Slice pork as thinly as possible across the grain and place a layer of slices on the base of a large container. Pour over some of the mango dressing. Layer more pork into the container and top with sauce. Chill until required.

Serve with salad and caramelised apples.

SERVES 10 TO 12

Marinated Chicken Breasts

½ cup low salt soy sauce
¼ cup medium dry sherry
½ teaspoon garlic, crushed
1 teaspoon ground cinnamon
½ cup cold tea
¼ teaspoon freshly ground pepper
2 tablespoons honey
1 teaspoon ANGOSTURA® aromatic bitters
6 x 150g chicken breast fillets

Combine all ingredients except chicken. Pour over chicken breasts and marinate for at least 2 hours in the refrigerator. Barbecue or grill for 2–5 minutes on each side or until cooked, basting occasionally with the marinade.

SERVES 4

Cold Spiced Cutlets

12 x 135g lean lamb cutlets
12 cutlet frills for serving

MARINADE

½ cup oil
1 medium onion, finely chopped
2 cloves garlic, crushed
2 teaspoons each ground cumin, ground ginger, grated fresh ginger
2 teaspoons Worcestershire sauce
1 cinnamon stick, broken into pieces
½ teaspoon paprika
1 teaspoon ANGOSTURA® aromatic bitters
2 teaspoons Dijon mustard
2 tablespoons fruit chutney
2 teaspoons curry powder
1 teaspoon salt

Trim cutlets. Combine marinade ingredients. Pour over cutlets and refrigerate, covered, for 24 hours, turning meat occasionally. Remove cutlets from marinade, grill or barbecue, cool on a rack and serve at room temperature with cutlet frills.

SERVES 6 TO 8

ANGOSTURA® aromatic bitters Scented Fruit

½ cup honey
1 tablespoon ANGOSTURA® aromatic bitters
2 cups diced rockmelon
2 cups strawberries
200g grapes
12 lychees

Warm honey with ANGOSTURA® and drizzle over fruit. Cover and chill overnight.

SERVES 6 TO 8

Light Christmas Pudding

60g fresh breadcrumbs
1½ cups skim milk
1½ tablespoons polyunsaturated margarine, melted
3 tablespoons ANGOSTURA® aromatic bitters
½ teaspoon Parisian essence
140g plain flour
2 tablespoons baking powder
½ cup Splenda brand sweetener
120g mixed dried fruit

Pour milk over breadcrumbs and allow to soak for 10 minutes. Stir in margarine, ANGOSTURA® and Parisian essence. Sift flour and baking powder into a bowl. Stir in Splenda and dried fruit. Stir wet ingredients into dry ingredients until well combined.

Coat a pudding basin with cooking spray and pour in mixture. Cover the top with foil and tie down with string. Place in a large saucepan and pour in hot water until halfway up the sides of the pudding basin. Bring to the boil, place the lid on the saucepan and simmer for 90–105 minutes or until cooked through.

Serve with custard.

SERVES 6

Lemon, Lime and ANGOSTURA® aromatic bitters Sorbet

¼ cup lime juice, sieved
¾ cup lemon juice, sieved
½ cup white wine
½ cup water
2 tablespoons ANGOSTURA® aromatic bitters
⅔ cup Splenda brand sweetener
2 egg whites
1 tablespoon caster sugar

Combine juices, wine, water and ANGOSTURA®. Stir in Splenda until dissolved. Pour into a metal tin and freeze until firm but not hard. In a clean bowl, whisk egg whites until stiff peaks form. Gradually beat in sugar until dissolved. Place frozen mixture into a separate bowl and beat briefly to break up ice crystals.

Fold ice mixture into egg whites and pour into metal tin and freeze solid.

TO SERVE: Scrape at the surface with a spoon to loosen ice crystals. Spoon into small bowls.

SERVES 8

Alfresco

Guacamole

½ cup finely chopped celery
crushed garlic and chilli, to taste
1 tablespoon lemon juice
¼ cup finely chopped onion
2 ripe avocados, mashed
2 teaspoons ANGOSTURA® aromatic bitters
2 tablespoons sour cream

Combine all ingredients in a bowl or food processor. Spoon into a serving dish and serve at once as a dip with corn chips.

SERVES 15 TO 20

Aromatic Potato Soup

2 onions or leeks, finely chopped
2 tablespoons ANGOSTURA® aromatic bitters
4 cups chicken or beef stock
1 sprig thyme
1 bay leaf
4 large washed potatoes, quartered
1 cup skim milk
chopped parsley

Simmer onions in ANGOSTURA® and stock until tender. Add herbs and potatoes and continue to simmer until potatoes are cooked. Cool slightly, purée in a food processor, adding milk. Reheat and serve, sprinkled with parsley and chives.

SERVES 4 TO 6

Gazpacho

8 large ripe tomatoes,
peeled, seeded and chopped
⅓ cup olive oil
¼ cup cider vinegar
juice of 1 lemon
1 clove garlic, minced
1 tablespoon ANGOSTURA® aromatic bitters
2 small onions, chopped
1 green capsicum, seeded and chopped
freshly ground pepper

GARNISH:
½ cup sliced spring onions, chopped
2 large cucumbers, chopped

Purée the tomatoes in blender. Place in a large bowl. Combine the remaining ingredients. Ladle the mixture, about 2 cups at a time, into the blender and blend until smooth. Combine with the tomato purée.

Chill and serve very cold, sprinkled with cucumber and spring onions.

SERVES 4

Pumpkin Soup

450g pumpkin, peeled and diced
3 cloves garlic, crushed
1 onion, chopped
30g margarine
500ml chicken stock
pinch of nutmeg or allspice
dash of ANGOSTURA® aromatic bitters
1 teaspoon light soy sauce
½ teaspoon white pepper
125–250ml milk

Sauté pumpkin, onion and garlic in margarine. Add chicken stock, nutmeg, ANGOSTURA® and soy sauce and cook until pumpkin is tender. Purée in blender. Thin soup with milk to desired consistency. Reheat and serve sprinkled with chopped parsley or chives.

SERVES 4 TO 6

Green Prawns with Crushed Spices

1kg green prawns
2 tablespoons ANGOSTURA® aromatic bitters
1 teaspoon coriander seeds
1 teaspoon cumin seeds
1 teaspoon mustard seeds
2 bay leaves, crumbled
1 teaspoon canned pink peppercorns, drained
2 onions, cut in to thin wedges
1 clove garlic, crushed
3 teaspoons finely chopped ginger
1 tablespoon olive oil
4 tomatoes, peeled and chopped
2 tablespoons lime or lemon juice

Peel prawns, leaving tails intact, and devein. Sprinkle with ANGOSTURA®, toss to coat, cover and refrigerate.

Grind seeds to a powder. Add peppercorns and bay leaves. Sauté onion, garlic and ginger in oil with spices until tender. Add tomatoes and lemon or lime juice. Simmer over low heat for 30 minutes or until onion is well cooked. Add prawns and stirfry in the spice mixture until just cooked. Serve at once with rice.

SERVES 6 TO 8

Variation: use a selection of seafood such as prawns, crab, calamari etc. Add some cayenne pepper for a more spicy dish.

Kenyan Style Chicken Tikka

8 chicken breasts on bone, halved

MARINADE
2 cups plain yoghurt
4 cloves garlic, crushed
2 teaspoons ground turmeric
3 teaspoons grated fresh ginger
1 teaspoon ANGOSTURA® aromatic bitters

Mix marinade ingredients, pour over chicken and refrigerate, covered, overnight. Remove chicken from marinade and barbecue slowly or bake at 180°C for about 25 minutes, dipping pieces frequently into marinade again so that a spicy crust builds up. Serve warm or at room temperature.

SERVES 6 TO 8

Eggplant Fritters with Yoghurt Sauce

1 cup plain yoghurt
¼ cup chopped chives
1 teaspoon ANGOSTURA® aromatic bitters
1 eggplant, approximately 500g
¾ cup self-raising flour
1 egg, lightly beaten
finely chopped chilli, to taste
oil, for frying
1 tablespoon ANGOSTURA® aromatic bitters

Combine yoghurt with 2 tablespoons of chives and 1 teaspoon of ANGOSTURA® in a bowl. Mix well together, cover and refrigerate until required. Prick eggplant all over with a fork, place on baking sheet and bake at 190°C for 45 minutes or until soft, turning once. Cool, peel, place in a bowl and chop to a coarse pulp with scissors. Work in flour, remaining chives, egg, chilli and 1 tablespoon of ANGOSTURA® to create a thick mixture. Refrigerate for at least 30 minutes then cook tablespoons of mixture in batches in hot oil until golden brown and crisp. Drain and serve with yoghurt sauce.

SERVES 4 TO 6 AS AN ENTRÉE

Stuffed Capsicums

ANGOSTURA®

6 green capsicums, blanched
seasoning, to taste
1 cup canned tomatoes, drained
1 cup fresh white breadcrumbs
2 teaspoons ANGOSTURA® aromatic bitters
1 egg, lightly beaten
3 tablespoons finely chopped onion
500g lean minced beef
½ cup grated cheddar cheese

Wash and dry capsicums. Cut a small slice from the side of each capsicum, removing seeds and membrane. Leave stem end intact. Combine egg, seasoning, onion, tomatoes, and half of the breadcrumbs in a large bowl and stand for a few minutes. Add beef and ANGOSTURA® and mix together well. Spoon meat mixture into capsicums and arrange in a greased baking dish in a single layer, open side up. Combine remaining breadcrumbs with cheese, sprinkle over capsicums and cover with foil. Bake at 180°C for 50 minutes or until cooked. Remove foil after 30 minutes to allow topping to brown.

SERVES 6

Fettucine with Artichoke Hearts and Pinenuts

4 sticks celery, chopped
3 cloves garlic, crushed
grated rind ½ lime or lemon
3 tablespoons butter or margarine
2 tablespoons ANGOSTURA® aromatic bitters
2 cups thickened cream
500g fresh white and green fettuccine
400g artichoke hearts
½ cup toasted pinenuts

Sauté celery, garlic and lemon or lime rind in the butter until tender. Add ANGOSTURA® and cream, bring to the boil, reduce heat and simmer to reduce slightly while cooking the pasta. Cook pasta in fast boiling salted water until just tender. Drain.

Halve artichoke hearts lengthwise and slice. Stir into sauce, add sauce to pasta, and heat through. Serve at once with pinenuts.

SERVES 6 AS AN ENTRÉE

Cajun Style Steaks with Fresh Fruit

MARINADE
2 tablespoons rum
2 cloves garlic
cayenne pepper, to taste
2 tablespoons ANGOSTURA® aromatic bitters
6 pieces of steak of choice, 2cm thick
freshly ground black pepper
2 mangoes, peeled, stoned and sliced

Combine rum, garlic, cayenne pepper and ANGOSTURA® in a bowl. Place steaks in a single layer in a shallow dish and pour over ANGOSTURA® mixture. Turn steak to coat, cover and refrigerate overnight, turning occasionally.

Barbecue or grill steaks to taste, basting them with marinade. Transfer to plate, grind black pepper over top and serve with slices of mango and or honeydew melon.

SERVES 6

ANGOSTURA® New Yorkers

6 x 150g New York cut steaks, trimmed of visible fat
1 teaspoon ANGOSTURA® aromatic bitters
3 tablespoons olive oil
2 tablespoons chopped dill
½ teaspoon black pepper
1 medium onion, finely chopped
4 tablespoons red wine
2 tablespoons chopped parsley
2 teaspoons mixed dried herbs

Place steaks in a single layer in a dish. Combine ANGOSTURA® with other ingredients in a bowl. Mix well. Pour mixture over steaks to coat. Cover and refrigerate for 2 hours. Barbecue steaks according to taste. Pour marinade into saucepan, bring to boil, reduce heat and simmer for 5 minutes or until onion browns and wine evaporates. Spoon over steaks and serve.

SERVES 6

ANGOSTURA® Beef Florentine

1 clove garlic, crushed
2 teaspoons olive oil
2 tablespoons ANGOSTURA® aromatic bitters
juice of ½ orange
6 x 125g lean steaks, trimmed of visible fat
steamed spinach
cherry tomatoes

Combine garlic, oil, ANGOSTURA® and orange juice. Coat steaks with marinade, cover and refrigerate for 2 hours. Grill or barbecue as required. Cut steaks into four slices and serve on a bed of spinach garnished with a cherry tomato.

SERVES 6

Italian Hamburgers

1kg lean mince beef
1 onion, finely chopped
2 cloves garlic, crushed
90g grated parmesan cheese
½ cup finely chopped parsley
2 eggs, beaten
1 teaspoon freshly ground black pepper
1 teaspoon ANGOSTURA® aromatic bitters
1 cup fine, fresh breadcrumbs
125g pinenuts
1 teaspoon dried oregano
1½ teaspoons salt
8 hamburger buns
shredded salad greens
sliced tomato

Place all ingredients, except buns and accompaniments, in a large bowl and mix gently but thoroughly with hands. Shape into 8 thick hamburgers and cook over hot coals for about 5 minutes on each side. Serve with shredded greens and tomato on buns.

SERVES 6 TO 8

Calypso Chicken

4 chicken breasts, boned
salt and pepper, to taste
1 clove garlic, crushed
1 teaspoon chilli, optional
pinch ground cumin
juice of 1 lemon
1 onion, sliced
2 green capsicums, finely chopped
4 tablespoons oil
1 teaspoon ANGOSTURA® aromatic bitters
1 teaspoon ground turmeric
2 tablespoons rum
300ml chicken stock
125ml thick coconut milk

Wash the chicken and season with salt, pepper, garlic, chilli, cumin and lemon juice. Marinate for 1 hour. Sauté onion and green capsicum in oil. Add chicken and cook until golden brown. Add the ANGOSTURA®, turmeric, rum, chicken stock and coconut milk, stirring well. Simmer on low heat for 30 minutes. Serve with plain boiled rice and a green salad.

SERVES 4

ANGOSTURA LTD.
ANGOSTURA®
aromatic bitters
ANGOSTURA
®
aromatic bitters
PRODUCTO DE TRINIDAD & TOBAGO
A skilfully blended aromatic preparation of gentian in combination with a variety of vegetable spices and vegetable colouring matter. Made with the same ingredients since 1824.
200 ml

Chocolate Mousse

50g semi-sweet chocolate, broken into pieces
125ml boiling water
25g icing sugar
2 teaspoons ANGOSTURA® aromatic bitters
4 egg yolks
4 egg whites

In a blender combine chocolate pieces, sugar, boiling water, ANGOSTURA® and egg yolks. Blend until smooth then cool to room temperature. Beat egg whites in a small bowl until stiff. Fold in chocolate mixture. Spoon into serving dishes, chill for several hours.

Garnish and serve.

SERVES 4

ANGOSTURA® Jubilee

1 x 300g packet frozen blueberries
1 x 300g packet frozen strawberries
1 x 300g packet frozen raspberries
juice of 1 orange
1 Granny Smith apple, peeled and cored
2 tablespoons brown sugar
2 tablespoons ANGOSTURA® aromatic bitters

Defrost frozen berries. Heat orange juice in frying pan over low heat. Stir in sugar and ANGOSTURA® until sugar dissolves.

Add apple and stir over moderately high heat until liquid has reduced to about 1 teaspoon. Reduce heat, add berries and stir until warmed through. Do not overcook. Add more sugar if desired.

Serve hot over ice cream or cold as breakfast or dessert.

SERVES 8

Island Style Bread and Butter Pudding

½ cup currants
1 tablespoon Coruba dark rum
½ large loaf day-old white bread (unsliced)
2 cups milk
1 ¼ cups thickened cream
3 tablespoons ANGOSTURA® aromatic bitters
2 eggs
¼ cup brown sugar
1 banana, sliced

Marinate currants in rum for at least 2 hours. Remove crusts from loaf and cut bread into 1cm cubes and place in a large bowl. Combine milk, cream and 3 teaspoons of ANGOSTURA®. Pour over bread and stand for about 5 minutes until nearly all the liquid has been absorbed.

Whisk eggs and sugar together until thick and creamy. Stir into bread with marinated fruit and the banana. Pour into well-greased baking dish and sprinkle with ANGOSTURA®. Bake at 160°C for about 1 hour or until firm. Turn off oven and let stand for 10 minutes.

Serve warm with scoops of ice cream sprinkled with ANGOSTURA®.

SERVES 6 TO 8

Caribbean
Cocktails

SHEER CHAMPAGNE CELEBRATION

(Created by John Sheer)

1 sugar cube
3 dashes ANGOSTURA® aromatic bitters
twist of orange rind
15ml Grand Marnier
15ml Hennessy cognac
chilled champagne

Drop sugar cube into chilled champagne flute and sprinkle with ANGOSTURA®. Add a twist of orange rind, Grand Marnier and cognac. Fill with champagne and serve.

CLASSIC MANHATTAN

1 dash ANGOSTURA® aromatic bitters
20ml Cinzano Rosso vermouth
30ml Canadian Club Classic

Stir ingredients into a margarita glass and garnish with a single cherry.

ELEPHANT WALK

30ml Gilbey's gin
20ml Jose Cuervo tequila
1 dash ANGOSTURA® aromatic bitters
orange juice
1 dash Grenadine

Mix gin, tequila and ANGOSTURA® in a highball glass, top with orange juice and sink a dash of Grenadine into the glass. Garnish with rockmelon and a cherry.

CARIBBEAN DELIGHT

25ml Malibu
15ml orange juice
15ml cherry brandy
1 dash ANGOSTURA® aromatic bitters
30ml pineapple juice
15ml Coruba rum
30ml lime or lemon juice

Combine all ingredients in a cocktail shaker with shaved ice. Serve in a chilled glass, garnished with an orange slice and a cherry.

GREYHOUND

45ml Smirnoff vodka
6 dashes ANGOSTURA® aromatic bitters
180ml grapefruit juice

Pour vodka over ice cubes in a tall glass. Fill with grapefruit juice. Stir. Add ANGOSTURA® and serve.

GINGER LIME FIZZ

40ml ANGOSTURA® aromatic bitters
twist of lime rind
40ml fresh lime juice
ginger beer

Place ice cubes in a glass, add lime juice and ANGOSTURA®. Fill with ginger beer, add the twist of lime rind and serve immediately.

ANGOSTURA® STAR

6 strawberries
60ml cream
30ml apricot nectar
1 dash ANGOSTURA® aromatic bitters

Blend all ingredients except cream and pour into a margarita glass. Use a toothpick to splay ANGOSTURA® into a star shape.

SWEET BITTERS CRUSH

30ml white rum
30ml Gilbey's gin
1 scoop crushed ice
30ml lemon juice
30ml Smirnoff vodka
30ml Cointreau
60ml pineapple juice
4 dashes ANGOSTURA® aromatic bitters

Blend all ingredients together in a blender except for the ANGOSTURA®. Place 4 dashes of ANGOSTURA® into a brandy balloon and add mixed ingredients. Garnish with pineapple and lemon wedges.

FORREST DELIGHT

(Created by Roweena Godenzi)

30ml Midori Melon Liqueur
15ml Galliano
15ml Cointreau
3 dashes ANGOSTURA® aromatic bitters
apple juice

Shake all ingredients and pour over crushed ice. Serve in a brandy balloon and garnish with sliced kiwi fruit and a strawberry.

INDEX

CASHBACK VOUCHER

The big ingredient in a little bottle

Receive $2.00 off the shelf price of ANGOSTURA® aromatic bitters when you purchase a bottle from your local bottle shop.
Simply cut out this voucher, attach your cash register receipt, fill in the details below and post it to:

ANGOSTURA® aromatic bitters
CASHBACK OFFER
LOCKED BAG 11
VILLAWOOD NSW 2163

NAME:...
ADDRESS:...
....
..........................**POSTCODE:**...........

Have you used ANGOSTURA® in cooking before? Yes ☐ No ☐
Would you like to receive more information on ANGOSTURA®?
Yes ☐ No ☐

There is no closing date for this offer.